The Super Veggies!

Hello there, Tiddlers! How are you?

I'm Mr Bloom, and this is my nursery.

Today I'm wearing a brand-new tank top, and it's very colourful indeed! Do you like it? It was a present from Granny Bloom. It's a bit different from my usual look, but I think it's always good to try something new!

Look at this strange vegetable I've grown in my allotment. Do you know what it is, Tiddlers?

It's called a kohlrabi and it's from the cabbage family. Can you say that word? **Cole-rah-bee**.

I wonder what it tastes like . . . Have you ever tried one? I can't wait to eat it when it's washed, peeled, chopped and cooked!

Now, let's go inside the nursery and I'll tell you a story all about trying new things.

Kohlrabi

One day, I found Colin dressed in his Captain Asparagus superhero outfit and reading a comic that had just been delivered. It was called *Super Spud and the Amazing League of Vegetables*.

"Oh, that looks like a good read, Colin!" I said, taking a peek at the pages. The story seemed very exciting!

"Super bean!" Colin cried. He really liked the new comic!

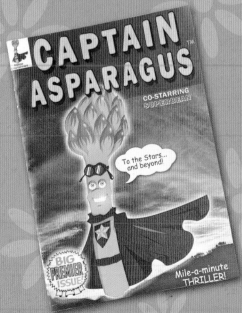

NEXT WEEK...

CAN SUPER SPUD
AND THE AMAZING LEAGUE
OF VEGETABLES SAVE
LADY PETRONELLA PARSNIP
FROM THE MOLTEN LAVA?

SUPER SPUD
and the
AMAZING LEAGUE
OF VEGETABLES!™

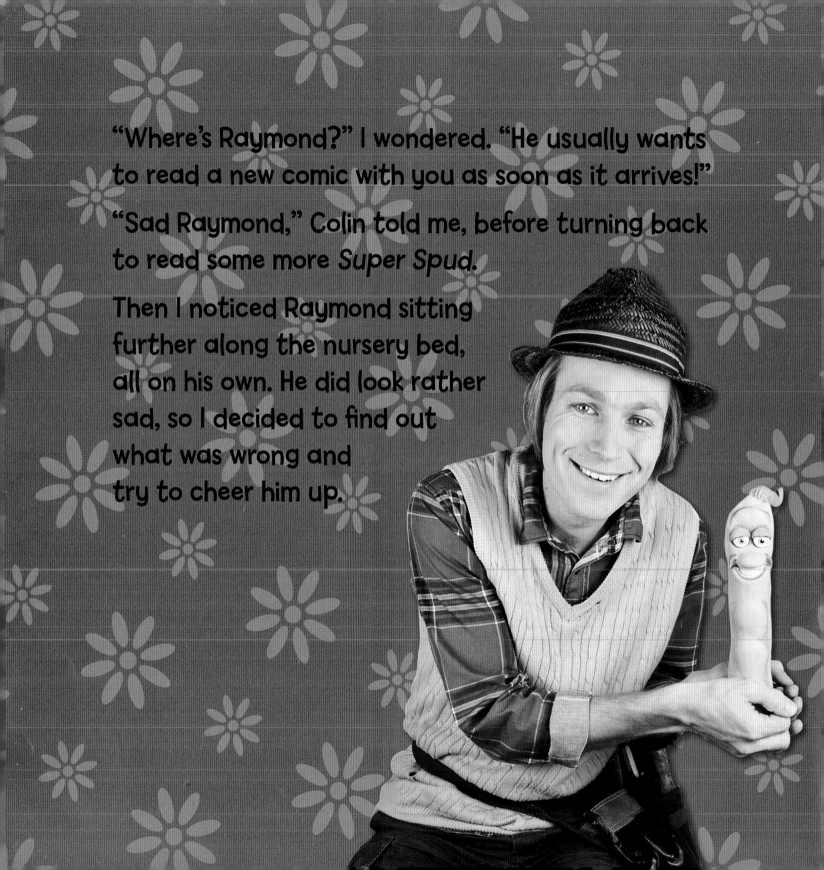

"Where's Raymond?" I wondered. "He usually wants to read a new comic with you as soon as it arrives!"

"Sad Raymond," Colin told me, before turning back to read some more *Super Spud*.

Then I noticed Raymond sitting further along the nursery bed, all on his own. He did look rather sad, so I decided to find out what was wrong and try to cheer him up.

"Hello there, Raymond! What's wrong?" I asked.

Raymond gave a really big sigh. "The postman delivered the wrong comic. I only like *Captain Asparagus*."

"That doesn't matter! It'll be good to try something new," I said. "I'm sure there must be something we can do to help."

Suddenly, Compo's fans began to **whirr** and his pipes started to **toot**. Lots of bubbles soon floated across the nursery!

What do you think he's got for us today, Tiddlers?

When Compo's drawer popped open, it was full of colourful costumes.

"Hey, it's superhero costumes from the *Super Spud* comic. Isn't that great!" I cried, holding them up. "Come on then, Veggies, who wants to try them?"

The other Veggies were excited and quickly got dressed up. Joan was the Incredible Curly Kale and wore a bright orange cape. Colin put on a shiny silver jetpack and became the Rocket Bean.

Margaret, with her twinkling tiara, was Cabbage Girl. And that left only Raymond.

"I think you should be Super Spud, Raymond. You're perfect for the part!" I told him.

"Really? Do you think so?" Raymond asked, with a little smile.

"Yes!" the other Veggies cried.

"Now you're all in your costumes, I'll read the comic aloud and you can all act it out," I said. "Are you ready, Super Veggies?"

Raymond still wasn't very happy, but he listened when I opened the comic and began to read.

"Oh no, Brave Aubergine has been captured by those sneaky Radish Rascals! Where have they taken him?" I said, and the Veggies gasped.

Sebastian, who was playing the part of Brave Aubergine, called to them from across the nursery. "Help me! Help me!" he cried.

"He's trapped in a cage and he can't escape," I continued. "What will happen to him? Will someone rescue him?"

"I can't fly," called Cabbage Girl, "so I can't save Brave Aubergine."

"I can't either," Curly Kale cried, "and Rocket Bean is too small. What shall we do?"

"There's only one thing for it. Super Spud must save the day!" I cried. "What about it, Raymond? Why don't you try something new and become Super Spud?" I suggested.

"OK!" Raymond said, finally joining in.

"Jump into your super-duper, supersonic aeroplane. You have to fly and save Brave Aubergine!"

I put Raymond in a plane from Compo's drawer. It had lightning bolts down the sides!

"The very sight of Super Spud arriving in his super aeroplane was enough to scare off the Radish Rascals. Brave Aubergine was finally free!" I read.

"Why, thank you, Super Spud," Sebastian the Brave Aubergine said. "To celebrate my escape, I think it is time for a song!"

Hey, Tiddlers, why don't you sing Sebastian's song? And we can all have a dance!

"It is good to try things that you have not tried before,

New things are exciting, so you must try them to be sure!

Raymond was a Super Spud – that was a job well done,

So I think we all deserve to sing and dance and have some fun."

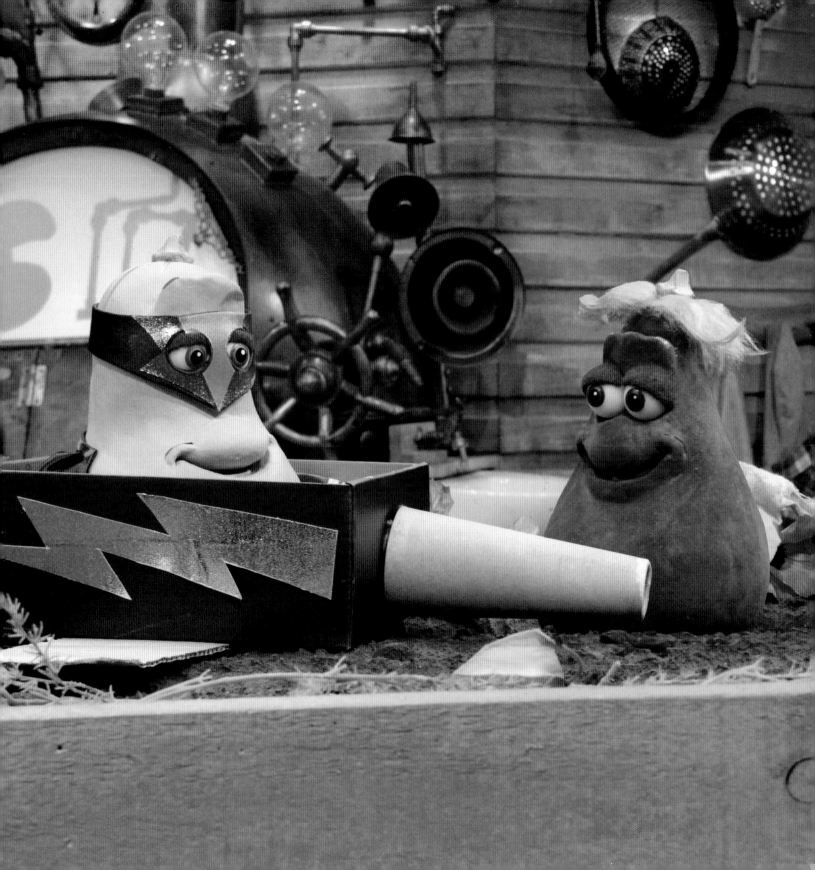

"Wasn't that fun!" I laughed. "So you see, Raymond, it's good to try new things."

"Yes, I will try new things from now on," Raymond said. "Look, Colin wants to be Super Spud, too!"

Colin makes a great Super Spud, don't you think, Tiddlers? And now it's time for me and the Super Veggies to say goodbye. We'll see you again soon for some more fun!

Goodbye bean!

MR BLOOM'S NURSERY: THE SUPER VEGGIES!
A BANTAM BOOK 978 0 857 51252 9

Published in Great Britain by Bantam,
an imprint of Random House Children's Publishers UK
A Random House Group Company.

This edition published 2013

1 3 5 7 9 10 8 6 4 2

Bantam Books are published by Random House Children's Publishers UK,
61–63 Uxbridge Road, London W5 5SA

www.**randomhousechildrens**.co.uk

Addresses for companies within The Random House Group Limited can be found at:
www.randomhouse.co.uk/offices.htm

THE RANDOM HOUSE GROUP Limited Reg. No. 954009

A CIP catalogue record for this book is available from the British Library

Printed in China

The Random House Group Limited supports the Forest Stewardship Council® (FSC®),
the leading international forest-certification organisation. Our books carrying the FSC label are
printed on FSC®-certified paper. FSC is the only forest-certification scheme supported by the leading
environmental organisations, including Greenpeace. Our paper procurement policy can be found at
www.randomhouse.co.uk/environment

MIX
Paper from
responsible sources
FSC® C020056
FSC
www.fsc.org